Seasons at Fenn Farm
The Winter Bond

By
Elle Hyde

PublishAmerica
Baltimore

PublishAmerica has allowed this work to remain exactly as the author intended, verbatim, without editorial input.

Hardcover 978-1-4512-3478-7
Softcover 978-1-4512-3479-4
PUBLISHED BY PUBLISHAMERICA, LLLP
www.publishamerica.com
Baltimore

Printed in the United States of America

This book is dedicated to my mother, Annette Kardos, who raised me to be sensitive to nature and show caring toward animals. If not for her, I would not be the lover of all things in nature that I am today.

I would like to acknowledge my husband, Mark Grosz, without whose guidance, tireless effort, and support despite my rebellion this book would not have been published.

The Winter Bond

Chapter One
First Snow

Every morning, I tried not to open my eyes before my internal alarm clock woke me at 7:00 am. If the prior night's weather forecast was remotely accurate, I would wake to bitter cold, disabling winds, and copious amounts of snow. The impending storm was the season's first Nor'easter headed up the North East Coast from North Carolina. It was greatly dramatized by the weather people, as it would blanket the East Coast days before Christmas.

After half an hour of shifting from side to side, I succumbed to the day's light. As I sat up, my eyes slowly focused on the window framing the woods surrounding my home.

"I love the first snow fall," I said with moderate enthusiasm.

Although the cold weather crippled my aging body and emphasized all that had fallen into disrepair, I was faithful in my staunch stance against becoming an exercise dinosaur. My walks in the fields and woods surrounding my home occurred regardless of the weather. With hesitant admission, I often put the walk off until day began to fade and the path and trees blended into the darkness. This morning was different. The first snowfall, especially during the Christmas season, was an inspiration to me.

I couldn't wait to breach the white canvas made of snow, leaving my footprints as evidence that I had ventured out into the world leaving my signature, although it would only last until the thaw or next snowfall. I often thought of footprints in the newly laid snow as a symbol of our life on earth delivered with beauty but nevertheless not permanent.

I dressed warmly and headed out the front door, grabbing my scarf as I opened the door to prepare for the unwelcoming wind.

Suddenly, I was entering a different world characterized by the distinct after effects of a fresh snowfall, still and quiet. The crows looked like lumps of coal against the panoramic white background. There was no auditory evidence of vehicles along the roads. My vision unveiled unblemished powdery snow dramatically transforming the woods into a magical landscape.

Thick layers of snow draped across the trees and enveloped the ground, masking all that lay beneath. There was no choice but to feel at peace with life in its simplicity and pulchritude. There was now a foreign feeling of all-consuming calmness and serenity at such a lonely time of year and at such an unresolved stage of my life. The trees, looking as though powdered sugar had been dusted on top of them, offered a continuous white buffer of peace and tranquility.

As I trudged up the path that traverses the woods, the snow crunched under the slight weight of my boots. My walking stick left uncommon circles in the snow just to the left of my footprints. I reached an opening that led into an abandoned neighboring corn field, and off in the distance, I noticed something on the ground. I squinted, attempting to bring what lay in my line of vision into focus. I could make out two brownish figures lying in the snow. I cautiously moved forward while attempting to maintain the quiet calmness that seemed to offer refuge to the figures.

As I crept closer, it became apparent that the figures were animals, one of which appeared to be a light brown, young female deer. The fawn was moving her head up and down as if licking the second figure, which did not appear to be a deer. I moved in closer, fixated on the second animal. I noticed white, brown, and black colored fur. As I approached even closer, the deer recoiled and immediately ceased contact with the second animal. I also stopped suddenly, tightening every muscle in my body to prevent further movement. After several moments of acknowledging my presence, the deer continued to care for the second animal. My presence did not appear important to her. This was a strange reaction from a deer during hunting season.

Overcome by curiosity and concern for the second animal, I remained frozen in my tracks until I felt I could advance farther without disruption. I was now within 15 feet of the two animals huddled together in the deep snow.

"It is a coonhound," I said to myself in disbelief at what my eyes and mind were deciphering. The young deer was licking the coonhound that lay motionless on the frozen ground. "What would cause a deer to befriend a coon hound?" I rhetorically thought to myself.

Although the young deer noticed my presence, she did not abandon the dog; instead, she continued to groom the dog's face.

"Please don't be dead. Oh, please don't be dead," I repeated to myself as if I could will away that which I did not want to witness.

As the distance between us shortened, the deer perked up her head and prepared herself for flight. I needed to continue my forward movement, although I knew it would scare away the fawn. I continued forward with slow, high steps, trying to keep my balance in the deep snow.

The young deer sprang up as I breached its comfort zone. She did not run; instead, she moved sideways with slow steps off her long thin legs, sinking into the snow almost to her knees. She did not run farther into the woods. She moved only a short distance away from the two of us, then lowered her head and remained very still, standing watch over the hound, alert to my every move.

I continued forward, bending down slowly toward the coonhound. It was partially covered in snow. Its back legs were motionless, seemingly frozen to the matted down snow that lay beneath its fur. I was not sure if the dog was alive or dead. I immediately wondered if it was some sort of hunting accident. That did not make sense to me though. I could not conceptualize the relationship between the hunted and what would be its prey.

"Please be alive," I continued to say to myself as I knelt down to examine the dog.

The dog was not dead; its eyes were opened and not glazed over. I noticed it was female. She was barely alive. There was no visible movement to her chest to show signs of breath. I slowly moved my hands around her fur investigating her body.

"Was she shot? Where is she injured?" I asked myself again and again.

The dog's head did not lift; her eyes remained focused off into the distance.

"Are you okay, dear?" I spoke out quietly to her.

She did not respond to my voice. I hadn't noticed the fawn's whereabouts at this point. I was fixated on the dog and trying to diagnose the condition that had rendered her motionless in the snow.

"I have to lift her up," I thought as I shifted my hands underneath her hind end and front shoulders. She was not large for her breed, which drew me to conclude that she was a young dog, not yet fully grown. As I slowly lifted her up, I felt the weight of her motionless body strike pain into my knees.

She allowed me to lift her, so I continued. I balanced her as best I could while kneeling on one knee. I was trying to keep her body off the ground so I could observe the snow underneath her for evidence of blood. The snow underneath was white with no signs of bodily fluids. I was relieved and my hope was restored. The only diagnosis I could make was that the young dog must've hurt one of her legs and at this point was lacking nourishment.

It was only at this time that I was relieved enough to shift my thoughts from the dog back to the fawn. I doubted her presence, but there she was, serving as assiduous watchdog from the same spot where she had moved to earlier. Her head was no longer positioned low; she was perked up watching my movements, almost in a protective manner.

I stood up with much effort and turned around back to the single footprints that had led me to the hound. As I slowly carried the dog back toward my house, I barely noticed the cold, the wind, or my aching body. I was consumed with concern for the dog. I wondered what would come of her.

"Will she live?" I asked myself as I continued to make my way down the hill, through the woods, toward my house.

"Why was she in the woods seemingly unharmed? Why was the fawn caring for her? Where was her owner? Had someone been out looking for her?" All my questions remained unanswered.

No part of this scene made sense to me.

Off in the distance, I could see the grey billowing smoke swirling upwards from my chimney.

"Oh, Thank God," I said aloud.

I could almost feel the warm, secure environment of my home. I was restored with energy and believed for the first time that the hound may survive the ordeal. I stopped the moment I realized that the sound of crunching snow beneath the weight of footsteps was not the only noise out there.

I turned my head to see the young fawn following us at approximately a ten-foot distance. When I stopped, she stood still. As I moved toward my house, so did she.

"She is trailing me," I said in disbelief.

I reached the imaginary border separating my yard from the woods. Only the sounds of the wind and the snow under my boots announced my presence.

Once again, I struggled to balance the dog on one knee as I reached out to grab the doorknob. Once inside, I laid the hound down on the rug at my front door. I stood up and looked out the window; peering out from the trees was the fawn staring at the house.

Chapter Two
Purpose

I covered the hound with a blanket and placed a bowl of water within her reach. I entered the kitchen and opened the pantry door, desperate for something to make for the weak, starving dog. I picked up a box of cereal.

"No, she won't eat this," I thought to myself.

I hadn't been responsible for feeding someone else for a long time. I grabbed a can of meat stew. My fingers could barely hold the can opener as I struggled to remove the lid from the can; they were still red with the sting of the elements. I emptied the stew into a bowl and laid it beside the water. I stood back and waited to see if she moved. She did not.

I stayed to observe her for a while; then I was forced to go on about my day, which turned into the next day, and the next day, and the next day.

Days passed and the dog grew strong, alert, and healthy. Oddly enough, she did not leave the front room where I had originally placed her.

"Maybe she is not comfortable with the surroundings," I thought.

I made the decision not to look for the owner until I was assured that she was going to be all right. She did not have a striking color or any identification tags. My closest neighbor was over a mile away. No one had come to my house to inquire as to her whereabouts. I wanted to believe that she was a stray and I kept this opinion, as it comforted me most.

I observed her improvement with great pride for having intervened at the right moment, at the right place, and at the right time. I purchased dog bowls and dog food from the local food store and took it for granted that she was in my house and life to stay.

It was not long before I had incorporated the presence of the coonhound into my daily life. She was loving, obedient, and kind. I noticed that her favorite place to lie was the entrance, so that was where I placed her bed.

She spent her days laying and looking out the front door—the same door that she entered, bringing her warmth, love, and safety. I did not spend time dwelling on what her life was like or where she came from before I found her. I was only concerned with her current life that was spent bringing me joy.

I did not purchase her a leash or collar; that seemed too permanent for me. In the back of my mind, her previous owner was going to step forward and claim her. When I let her out of the house, I placed a doubled up clothes line rope looped around her neck to form a makeshift collar. When she came back in, I removed it.

I had not named her, as nothing had come to mind yet; although I had many thoughts about a proper and fitting name. She evoked in me a sense of love and belonging. I was restored with energy for the first time in a very long time; I was taking care of another being and sharing my home and my heart. I was not lonely.

"What a wonderful Christmas present," I often said to myself.

I was given the gift of unconditional love.

I was given the gift of companionship and purpose.

Chapter Three
Many Levels

Snow fell throughout the night, leaving yet another layer of snow on the ground to add to the existing inches of powder.

I awoke to the hound howling for me to let her out. I did not hesitate to get out of bed these last few mornings. I moved with quickness, uncommon for my stiff joints at this hour. I grabbed my robe, shuffled my feet into my slippers, and descended the steps to feed her. This had become my morning ritual.

She sat in the hall on the same rug, looking out the window this morning. She was howling at the fresh blanket of snow. I looked out the window to view the standard crows, barn sparrows, and squirrels. Nothing appeared out of the ordinary.

"What do you see out there that I don't, girl?" I asked her.

I walked past her and placed my hand on the door handle. She stood patiently as if telling me she would wait. I opened the door this day without restraining her. I felt confident that she had grown accustomed to the house, as she was not acting hyper.

"Go out, girl," I said to her with encouragement.

She looked up at me and paused. She wagged her tail and for the first time, licked my hand.

"Go on, go out. Then we'll have breakfast," I said to her as I rubbed her ears. She had soft large ears that felt like flannel.

Out the door, she ran with quick, precise steps. For the first time now, I became alarmed and concerned that she would run away. I immediately followed her without a care that I was in my robe and slippers.

I could see her black figure running toward the path to the woods.

"No, girl!" I called out to her. "No, girl!" I shouted louder.

She was howling with every step as she ran toward the woods. My heart sank, as I felt overwhelming fear that I would not get her back into the house. What if I was never able to find her again?

I stopped suddenly and my eyes widened with great doubt and surprise at what I saw. The young fawn sprang from the woods as if she had been there all along. The hound wagged her tail with fierce resolve. Her long ears pinned back as she uncontrollably licked the young deer. The doe stood with all four legs spread out, positioning herself closer to the ground, aiding contact with her reunited partner, all while allowing her to lick her face.

Suddenly, the two disappeared into the trees. I was still too surprised and shocked to comprehend what had just happened. She was gone.

Soon enough, the realization overcame my shock. I felt the cold air suck the breath out of my lungs. There I stood, alone. I was feeling another emotion for the first time in years; however, this time, it was not fulfillment but loss. My eyes overfilled with tears expressing my pain. The cold air bit at my wet cheeks. I fought to stay focused on the tree line as it became harder to see. I could still hear her howling. I strained to focus on the blurred figures on the meandering trail as the two ran up the hillside. I could not dismiss the sheer unadulterated look of joy they manifested at the reunion. The dog's throaty howl now drew faint as the figures disappeared over the top of the hill. Once I could no longer hear her voice, I turned away. I felt sadness over my lack of true companionship; however, I also felt the stronger pull of emotion toward the beautiful bond between these two mismatched souls. As I reached out to turn the doorknob, a snow flake descended down from the grey sky, swirling and floating to finally rest on my skin. Then as I blinked, it was gone, melted from the heat of my arm. I could not help but think of the symbolism.

Like the fleeting life of the snow that began to fall, it was not long before my friend's footprints would be erased.

My emotions, much like the events of the last week of my life, consumed my thoughts. I worried about the winter months ahead and the fate of the dog that had already succumbed to malnutrition. My fear was abated when I re-envisioned their inspirational reunion. It was not entirely clear who took care of whom, or which of the two felt more alone during the hound's confinement.

I now believe that the heart bonds without or despite our mind's intervention. Love magically reassures us, comforts us, and pushes us to transcend bias and adversity.

"She will always be a part of me," I thought. Then a smile appeared upon my lips as I announced to myself, "What an ethereal Christmas gift I was given."

Spring Thaw

Chapter One
Angel

The long suppressive winter was ending. The lemon colored crocus fought the stiff soil and peaked through the last of the remaining snow. I washed the few dishes that had collected in the sink and looked out the window into the stifled garden.

"I wonder if it will be warm enough today to work outside in the garden," I thought to myself. It was early in the year, but I had always started my gardening early, despite the weather. It was what saved me from cabin fever.

I gazed at my reflection in a porcelain plate. I saw me looking back at me. I saw me, ironically, with a porcelain glaze. I was older, more tired and cynical, but I was wiser. I looked away as if horrified at my appearance. But I was not horrified at my appearance, just disappointed with the rate at which my energy was fading. I recognized the beauty—the inspiring beauty—surrounding me. Yet I felt as though I was mugged. I always changed my focus when faced with acceptance—acceptance of the natural course of my life.

"Enough. Okay, I'll start by raking the leftover fall from the herb garden, and then maybe skim the leaves out of the pond," I thought as I started making a mental list of the first spring thaw chores that I performed every year. My mind shifted from the preparation of the gardens to the soft fur that I felt along the back of my legs.

"Angel, what do you want?" I turned and picked up the large grey cat that was begging for attention. Angel was a cat-sitting project that I was currently carrying out.

"You already had your breakfast," I said to him as I stroked his thick fur. "Here, I'll give you some more crunchies." Crunchies was the word I used to refer to the rock hard dried cat food that Arlene had asked me to feed him.

Arlene was a neighbor and a dear friend. She had gone on vacation, as was standard at this time of year, and I always welcomed the opportunity to watch him. Angel was a very loving, friendly cat that I found as a kitten in my barn. I did not want to keep him myself, as I had never been much of a cat person. Though, I admit that watching him a couple times a year was quite enjoyable for me, and it was enough cat exposure to satisfy my desire to have a cat.

I turned and opened the pantry and removed the bag of food that had arrived with him. It was only the third day of his six-day stay with me and the bag was significantly smaller than it had been when he was dropped off. I had a habit of overfeeding him, much to Arlene's dismay. He was always returned to her healthy, content, but heavier.

As I lifted the bag from the shelf, Angel took a large bouncing leap toward the bowl that lay in the corner. He purred with anticipation as if he had not eaten in days. The truth was he had just eaten an hour ago.

"Angel, you're turning into quite a piglet," I said to him as he began crunching the small brown cat shaped morsels.

I turned and made my way toward the door. I picked up my thick brown coat off the tree rake and the scarf that hung beneath it. Then I tied the scarf around my neck, and as I did so, I did not notice Angel moving toward the door. He was standing behind the wooden antique saltbox that sat in my entrance hall. I pulled my gloves onto my hands and reached for the doorknob. As I opened the door, an unexpected gust of chilling wind blew through the door. I turned my face from the draft and turned my attention back toward the coat rake to grab a hat, and as

I focused on the brown knit cap, I didn't notice Angel run through the open door.

I tugged at the knit cap, pulling it down over my ears. Once it was in place, I continued through the doorway without a clue that Angel was now on the outside.

I made my way to the barn to gather the necessary gardening tools. I observed the dried brown autumn leaves that covered the new spring growth. Now wet and heavy, they threatened the rebirth of my gardens, the woods, and trees. I thought of the cycles of life that were perpetuating before my very eyes. "I can't stop it, nor can I change it. Just I can't change the course of my aging." I continued to immerse myself in philosophical thoughts. "If I am so intuitive, why do I struggle with the cycle and changes within my own body?" This I could not answer.

After this final thought, I turned and focused back on the corner of the barn that housed my tools. I gathered a rake, wheelbarrow, and skimmer, and left the barn. As I walked toward my pond, only then did I notice the chilled air. "It's cold out here for this time of year," I thought as I set the wheelbarrow down on its rusty legs. I looked into the pond, surveying the task ahead. I picked up the skimmer and began cleaning it. As I pushed the water around, my thoughts began to wander once again. The floating leaves slowly drifted into the corner, exposing the dark murky water that lay beneath them, swishing with the current from the skimmer. "It will soon be summer, then fall, winter, and once again, I will perform the same chore. The natural beauty that surrounds me is worth it." I convinced myself without defiance as I scooped them up and slammed the skimmer into the wheelbarrow.

A loud squeal stopped my actions and I stood still, straining and waiting to see if I would hear it again. Then I heard the same high-pitched screech again. "What is that?" I assumed that it was some kind of cry. I turned suddenly to see Angel quickly prancing down the yard toward the house. I did not have time to be surprised at the fact that he was outside and not inside where he belonged. There, again, I heard the high-pitched scream. I then focused on the object in Angel's mouth. The legs of the small creature dangled with every step Angel took. The small animal was white, black, and light tan. I dropped the rake and ran toward him.

"Angel, drop it!" I screamed at him. He did not break pace. I turned and ran back to the skimmer. I picked it up frantically. I turned and ran toward him again, screaming, "Angel, drop it!"

Angel was obviously not accustomed to the tone of my voice or the swinging object being wielded around his head. He dropped the animal. I cast the skimmer aside and knelt down to observe the small, petrified animal.

I immediately untied the scarf from around my neck and tossed it over the animal's head in an attempt to shield him from his surroundings. I was not sure if it was a mouse or some other rodent. It appeared too large to be a mouse. Regardless, I was concerned for its life.

As I picked up the small animal, I held it to my chest.

"Shhhhhh…It will be okay. Hold on, honey," I said in an attempt to calm it.

I reached my door and turned the knob as I sheltered the small animal. Once inside, I placed the scarf enveloping the animal down on the kitchen counter and slowly pried it apart.

There before my eyes was a baby rabbit, so young its eyes hadn't yet opened, and its ears were so small, it was the size of a deer mouse. I could only imagine the sheer terror it must have felt.

"Angel must have found a nest and picked him from it," I thought. Rabbit warrens were very common in my gardens at this time of year. They did not fall to predators though, as I did not have a dog or cat. I saw my yard as a sanctuary for the wild life that inhabited it.

"I need to find its home," I said as I wrapped it up again in the scarf. I walked to my cabinet and grabbed a large pot with high sides to shelter the baby. I placed the bunny, still wrapped in the scarf, inside the pot and turned to go outside and look for the warren.

I searched my gardens without luck.

"Oh, Angel, where did you find it?" I said aloud as I ran from garden to garden frantically searching for the rabbit's nest.

After realizing that I was not going to find it, I ran back to the house with one thought on my mind: ascertaining whether the fragile baby bunny was hurt.

"I don't know how to care for a baby bunny," I thought to myself. "They rarely live without their mother. I've heard about how sensitive their systems are. I don't want this baby to die." These many thoughts flooded my mind.

I opened the door and again thought of Angel. "Oh my god, I left the bunny inside with Angel!" As I was not accustomed to the habits of a cat, I had not thought of the cat once again hunting the rabbit.

I ran into the house and immediately the pot was in my field of vision. I did not see Angel. I reached the pot and looked down with panic still stirring in my stomach. "Thank God," I said as I viewed the pan and the scarf moving slightly from the baby that lay within it.

"What am I going to feed it?" I wondered. "I have no clue."

I stopped and stretched my hands toward the floor. "I've got to calm down here and think logically. I need to get an eyedropper and some warm milk." I was now thinking with forethought instead of mere reaction.

I opened my bathroom medicine cabinet and searched for an eye dropper. "Oh, where the hell is it?" I was again becoming flustered. I did not know where Angel was. "How am I going to care for this bunny and Angel at the same time in my small house? Calm down; put the bunny in your bedroom; go online;and see what you are supposed to feed this bunny," I said as I practiced my yoga deep breathing technique. I picked up the baby and placed a soft kiss on top of his brownish, blackish fur.

I soon learned that the sustenance the bunny needed was grass, greens, and the newly sprung buds from the trees waking from their winter's sleep. I took up the responsibility of becoming the baby's mother. I held, fed, sheltered, and immensely bonded with and subsequently loved this small dependent gift of nature. I also felt a responsibility, as Angel had disjointed this fragile young life from her birth mother. The week that Angel and the bunny spent as cohabitants of my house was very stressful. I was never as happy as when Arlene picked Angel up. I told her about his great escape and rampage. She apologized for the actions of her loving pet, although we both knew that his actions were instinctual and not mischievous. As easily as he had been dropped off, he left, leaving me alone with my new dependent.

Chapter Two
Release

It seemed like yesterday that Angel captured the baby bunny, and here it was weeks later and I was proudly releasing her back to her rightful place in the wild.

"Are you ready to go and live your life?" I asked her as she peered at me from behind the toilet. "You are going to feel the grass, dirt, and run and jump," I said to her as I knelt down in front of the toilet to pick her up.

She did not become too tame during her tenure with me. She recognized me as the one who fed her, but not as a source of comfort. She was the size of a coffee mug. Her ears had white tips and were larger now than they were the day Angel brought her to me. She no longer looked like a mouse; she looked like a small bunny.

As I reached out to her, she tried to run away.

"Come on, don't run today of all days. You want to go free," I said to her.

It was a sad day for me. I found such joy in caring for her. I flourished just as she did with each day that she survived, and not only did she survive, she grew strong.

As I grasped at her and picked her up, I held her close to my chest. I always placed her there hoping that she would hear my heart beat and think of her own mother.

"Sshhh, don't be scared." I carried her through my bedroom and down the stairs. I did not stop to put on a coat, although the air was very cold that morning.

I wanted to put her out in the morning so she could feel the grass, leaves, and sticks. I wanted her to be in her surroundings before nightfall. I tried to keep her habits nocturnal, but feared that if I let her out at night, she would fall prey that first night.

I could not help but start to tear up. Although I knew this day would always come, it did not make it easier.

I walked her past the pond and to the edge of the woods where the yard and trees met. I kissed her on the white triangle of fur on her forehead, knelt down, and spoke one last time to her.

"I love you. Be safe and be strong."

In the same amount of time it had taken Angel to steal her from her nest, she was gone. She ran into the woods and under some low-lying brush. Her eyes were large and her nose constantly twitching; she was looking at me. Although these surroundings were foreign to her, she seemed comfortable in them. I did not say anything else to her. I couldn't. I didn't know what to say; goodbye was too sad.

I turned and my teary eyes progressed to complete sobbing. I brushed away my tears and felt a true sense of loss.

I walked past the pond to the barn to get the skimmer and finish the task of removing the leaves from the pond. I pushed aside yard tools and picked up gloves, a bucket, the skimmer, and the wheelbarrow. I backed the wheelbarrow out of the barn and through the yard to the pond.

When I reached the pond, I could not divert my thoughts from my baby bunny.

"What is she doing? Is she okay?" I asked myself without knowing the answer and knowing I never would.

I grabbed the skimmer and turned to start removing the leaves from the pond. In the water floated a small round object.

"What did Angel do now?" I immediately blamed him, as during that short housebreak, he had wreaked such havoc.

I looked closer and discovered that the object was a baby bunny.

I was physically sick.

"NO!" I screamed, "NO, NO, NO!" I could not believe my eyes. "Did she follow me after I left her off in the woods? She would not know what a pond was, what water would do to her." I wondered if I had failed her, raising her in such a sheltered environment.

I strained every muscle within my frame to reach the skimmer out to the floating body of the baby that I had just released and had grown to love. At that second, the necklace that I had worn around my neck for countless years, for lack of reason, fell from my neck and into the cold dirty pond water.

"Oh my GOD!" I cried as I grasped at the necklace that had come loose. There was no time to choose between the baby rabbit and the cherished necklace. I watched as the gold medallion floated down below the murky water until it was no longer visible. Without hesitating, but while pushing the water with the skimmer closer to the edge of the pond, I thought of the warm sun hanging overhead, warming my body and heart. I could still hear the music and see his face as he asked me to choose between his left and right folded fist. I chose the left and he turned his fist to display the antique gold medallion. As tacitly as the memory had appeared, it disappeared as I realized that the bunny was now within reach of my skimmer.

I reached out to lift the limp and lifeless body onto the head of the skimmer. Gently, I moved the skimmer out of the water and closer to me. I looked with tears in my eyes as I viewed the tiny face that had come to represent love, belonging, and purpose to me during those last weeks.

"She was gone only minutes. Why would this happen? What is the reason for this?" I screamed the words within my mind. "I cared so much for this baby and she should have gone to live a full life." I could not remove the grotesque vision from my mind of the baby feeling the grass under her paws for the first time, running free and then struggling to find her footing as she sunk into the abyss of the pond. I placed the skimmer on the ground and dropped to my knees. I sobbed aloud as I stroked the bunny's soaked fur.

The next hours were consumed with grief, unanswered questions, and flashes of painful losses from my past. It seemed that this one event opened a floodgate of painful memories. I remembered all the loss that had neither rhyme nor reason.

I carried the baby in my hands to my rose rock garden and buried her amongst the bleeding hearts and ferns. My hands were cold, but I made it a point to bury her deep enough.

"I cannot bear to see her dug up by some nocturnal animal," I thought as I dug deeper until I was more than a foot beneath the soil.

Once she was buried, I stood and stood, arching my back and rubbing my lower back as I stretched. The chill was taking its toll on my joints. I turned and walked toward the shelter of my home.

The day soon gave way to night and I walked up the stairs to my bedroom drinking a glass of red wine to dull my pain. I set the wine on my nightstand and pulled back the blanket. I looked at it and once again, another memory of loss came to me.

"I remember how much Mother loved to crochet. She sat on the couch with her knitting needles with a large bag of yarn on the floor beside her. I miss you, Mom." I stroked the blanket, speaking aloud as I often did to her. I felt a sense of ease that she could hear me. I had spent so many years at odds with her. I tried my best to amend the past during the last few years of her life, caring for her when she was overtaken by dementia.

I slipped my feet between the chilled sheets, slid my body down, and placed my head on my pillow.

"Why did this all have to happen?" I thought as I turned out the light. "Once again, here I am," I was now holding my forehead. "I ultimately cannot control the outcome of life, of my relationships. I can try my best to make a difference, to bring my love into that relationship, but if nature or God has a different course set, despite my pain, grief, or effort, I cannot change it." These were words that I had spoken to myself and said aloud to my friends many times. This night, they did not bring me any closer to acceptance.

I closed my eyes and suddenly remembered my necklace.

"I won't get it back. It will stay lost. I want it to be lost just like I lost my bunny. Let it lie beneath the water and be buried just like the baby I buried today." I thought this would somehow make it all right.

"All I can do is try—try and work to except the consequences of the meaningless actions in this screwed up life."

Then I shut my eyes and soon fell asleep.

Chapter Three
Mother Nature's a Bitch

The next morning, I opened my eyes and looked out the east window of my bedroom. The nourishing spring sun popped over the hills early that morning. I looked at the clock and noticed it was an hour earlier than my normal rising time. I got out of bed and made my way down the stairs to the kitchen to make a pot of coffee.

"Ah, the smell of coffee in morning makes it the start of day." I poured a cup and took a sip.

I turned and stood at the window gripping the cup of hot coffee. Outside, the day was promising to be clear and bright. The grass was coated in frost, each blade with crystal tipped edges. Young robins stood on the fence posts watching the other birds in the aviary community forage, sing, and gather old leaves and twigs to build new spring nests. The chickadees soared and swooped over the pastures as the crows sat high in the trees with their usual commanding presence.

I gazed out the window beyond the pond in an act of avoidance. I noticed a bunny in the distance. I could not tell how big it was. I tried to focus my eyes on the figure.

"That bunny is TINY. It couldn't be, could it?" I thought to myself in sheer disbelief. "It could be. I never saw her run into the pond; maybe it is. I don't know that the drowned bunny was mine."

I attempted to convince myself of the many possibilities. My spirits lifted as I continued to watch the young rabbit and all the new life budding, growing, and thriving around her.

"This is how it should be," I thought, as though this bunny was mine, and then as soon as I was somewhat convinced, it ran closer to the house, and I saw that it was much larger, older.

"Mother Nature is a bitch," I said aloud. "I will never agree or like it; the strongest of the fittest is a bunch of shit. What about the weak?"

The thought was neither here nor there; I was accepting the outcome of the previous day's events, but voicing my dislike of them. I refused to overlook the beauty or the tragedy that comes with springtime. I also refused to dismiss or ignore the memories of our lives back in the springtime of our lives.

I walked back upstairs to dress to go outside to fish my necklace out of the pond and place it back where it belonged.

"On my neck," I said aloud. I then concluded, "Maybe we need memories of loss to remind us how far we, I've, come." I smiled and was once again at peace in my natural environment.

Summer Monarch's

Chapter One
Camille's Acquaintance

Spring's chilling air quickly gave way to the long sunny days and bright starry nights of summer. This night was particularly clear. The sky appeared as a blue shroud spotted with pinholes of light. The sounds of summer were particularly audible, overlapping with varying calls. The field crickets competed with the throaty calls of the bullfrogs that inhabited the surrounding ponds. As I lay awake by the open window, listening to the nighttime serenade, the fireflies in the distant fields flickered with twinkling lights. Summer nights were full of life as compared to the other seasons on the farm, which were characterized by silence or the sounds of predators overtaking their prey piercing through the stillness. The cries of the hunted were unnatural and haunting sounds that often awoke and disturbed me. Summer nights comforted me.

"I am eager to start my manicured beds," I thought to myself as I went through the checklist of the chores I needed to do the next morning. "I will start by weeding the butterfly garden."

This garden was my favorite. Thoughts of my childhood were synonymous with summer more so than any other time of year. Days consumed with play with my sister, Lee, always surfaced when I thought of summer. Lee loved the butterflies' orange and yellow colors fluttering in the fields. She called them color flies.

I erected a mental barrier to protect me from any unpleasant thoughts that might penetrate my mind when I thought of Lee, the summer, or the Monarchs she called color flies.

"We used to sit on the concrete floor playing jacks for hours," I thought as I smiled and let myself laugh for a second when I recalled the series of short songs we used to sing while we played.

I fell asleep to this pleasant thought and woke early the next morning to the calls of the birds chirping and singing to one another.

"Up and out," I said aloud as I began the series of morning rituals with the intent to not waste any time. Ceasing the opportunity to work in the cool morning air was welcomed, as within hours, the air would become too humid for gardening.

As I sat on the outside step of the back porch and drank the last of my coffee, I looked out at the hundreds of trees that so suddenly abandoned their gray and brown foliage for overnight bursts of a kaleidoscope of greens. The fields were blooming with milkweed and an abundance of nature's wild flowers. The gardens surrounding my house were filled with tall, soft, colored flowers framing the grounds with beauty. I looked down at the ground and spotted the many weeds choking out the healthy soil.

"Time to go to work and battle these weeds," I thought as I took my last drink and set the mug on the step as I stood and stretched. My hands braced my lower back, "I hope to get in a few hours before my back aches too much."

Despite my body's best efforts to persuade me to give up the heavy gardening I so much enjoyed, I went out every morning to perform some sort of ground control to stave off the insurgent weeds.

The small chickadees descended from the trees to the ground in clusters with seeming bursts of commotion as they fought for the seed scattered about. I encouraged the proliferation of birds by offering several feeds for all varieties. I adored the many birds that made my farm their home during the summer months. I particularity loved the barn swallows with their bat-like wings and quick movements as they flew out the windows and openings of the barn.

I gathered my tools and had just knelt down to start weeding when I heard the stones on the driveway clap together, signaling that someone was walking down the long winding drive to the farmhouse. A fleeting stab of fear overcame me as I felt the shock of a stranger's sound intruding my safe space.

As I turned my head, the sun prevented me from viewing the stranger, although I attempted to shield the rays from my eyes with my right hand. I strained harder to recognize the stranger, hoping that it would be one of several of the usual visitors: mail carrier, a parcel delivery person, or a meter reader. Summer seemed to encourage visitors to approach the house more so than other seasons, which offered challenging conditions to dissuade them from walking up the drive.

I stood up with my hand still to my brow, my heart now pounding inside my chest.

"Sophie," the stranger called out my name.

"Hello?" I replied with hesitation, not recognizing the voice and still straining to bring the stranger into focus. I concluded that the voice belonged to a man, but I did not recognize it.

"Hello," he reached out his hand, "my name is Francis. I hope I did not startle you."

But the intrusion had startled me. I was also hesitant and curious as to who he was and why he was at the farm. I quickly made several assessments.

"He does not have a uniform on. He is wearing faded baggy jeans, brown colored climbing shoes, and a faded tee shirt. He is not here on professional business," I thought as I continued to process his appearance. Then I answered his question. "No, not at all, although I have to admit, I am curious as to whom you are." I did not smile as I turned my body to block out the sun so that I could look at his face. I was now very uncomfortable and the stress was mounting within me.

"I was hoping I could photograph your woods," he said as he held up the camera that hung around his neck. "Camille sent me."

Camille was a close friend of mine who had the annoying unyielding habit of setting me up with younger men.

I began feeling slightly more comfortable for the first time in his presence. My close friend would have performed a very thorough background check of any possible mating candidate. I did not want to be rude, but equally, I did not want to engage in a conversation that would lead him to believe that I was remotely interested in having a male acquaintance.

"Well, I am at a disadvantage here, Francis," I continued to awkwardly smile as I spoke, "but Camille, my dear loving friend, did not tell me you were coming." I spoke with clear sarcasm. "She has a tendency to do this to me."

"I am sorry. Do you want me to leave?" he asked in a very concerned and defeated tone.

"No, not at all, but please tell me why you want to photograph my woods," I asked him, trying awkwardly to engage in lighthearted conversation. This form of communication with strangers was foreign to me.

"I am actually an artist. I photograph nature, then wash out the image and watercolor it. I met Camille at a gallery opening last month. When she saw my work, she said your farm would be the perfect place for me. I am surprised she did not inform you that I would be coming."

"I'm not," I said with a smile. "It is a beautiful, inspirational place, so I do understand why she offered my farm up to be your muse." I spoke to him very cordially, but again, without any injection of a personal tone that he could possibly misinterpret. "You are welcomed to photograph the woods; I would love to claim ownership of them, but would not be so bold as to challenge the current owner's wrath."

"Oh, who would that be? Do I need to have written consent to trespass?" he asked with concern.

"No, I am sure Mother Nature will allow you to trespass," I replied. We both laughed at that one moment of levity. For the first time, I was able to relax and breathe. He was no longer a stranger to me.

"Feel free, Francis, on one condition," I said.

"Thank you," he replied. "And what is the condition?"

"That you allow me to see your art once you are done," I said, smiling a confident and witty smile.

"I think that can be arranged, Sophie," he said as his smooth white perfectly aligned teeth reflected the sun behind me.

I smiled back, but with much less dramatic efficacy. I turned and returned to my weeding. The weeds were much less resilient than I had originally thought. The ground was not as hard on my knees, or was it that I was paying less attention to petty inconveniences and was now preoccupied with much more pleasant thoughts?

Chapter Two
The Sheltering Fields

The conversation I had with the photographer resounded in my mind, resonating over and over until I feel asleep that night. When I awoke, the vision of his frame and kind eyes appeared in my mind.

"This is not like me," I thought to myself as I tried to reason away my enamored reaction to him. Fenn Farm was my comfort zone and had always provided a buffer of security. To be so taken in by a stranger within my zone of security had never happened before.

The morning routine was inconsequential as I drifted between the hours that took me to noontime.

"I have to get my head together," I said, chiding my lack of organization.

I began to shovel my car keys, checkbook, and wallet into my purse. I continued to review the list of tasks that I had mentally set out for myself.

"I have a thousand and one chores to do before five," I said as I looked at the clock and ushered myself toward the door.

I began exiting the house with my purse slung over my shoulder, and reached into the large satchel to find the keys that I had just dropped into it. I stepped out the door and onto a small orange envelope.

"Oops," I said as I lifted my foot back up and off the envelope.

The relatively small envelope was placed perfectly on the middle of the first step.

"What's this?" I thought as I bent down to pick up the envelope. "I did not hear anyone come up the drive or at the door. I wonder when this was placed here, and by whom?"

I turned the bright orange envelope over and lifted the flap. The color reminded me of the bright orange contrast against the black wings of the Monarch butterfly. The color and meticulous writing of my name should have given me a hint as to identity of the author. Regardless, my curiosity was peaked. I pulled a heavy linen card out of the envelope. The card was of the same color.

The note read,

Whether through instinct or if by words, everyone at first introduction is a stranger. Let us be strangers no more, Sophie. Meet me for lunch today under the summer sun amongst the tall grasses of your in your back yard. 2:00. Regrets only: 810-237-8900.

F.R.

My entire being sparked with excitement, as if I was a teenager again. My face, I imagined, was blushed as I lifted the note upwards and to my lips. I paused and allowed myself a moment of elation before I turned and sat on the step.

"Oh my God. What do I do? This is crazy," I uttered aloud.

I was overrun with a rush of happiness. I acknowledged to myself that this was an emotion that I had not experienced in years.

"Is it that he is thinking the same way? He must. Why would he invite me to a picnic if he didn't? I wonder what he thinks of me. I wonder if he's replayed our brief conversation over and over in his head as I have. This is crazy. Get a grip, woman."

My emotions swung from joy to fear to self-condemnation.

"What do I wear?" I asked as I suddenly stopped my thoughts. "Wow, I have lost the plot here. I need to just calm down. I will go back into the house and regroup." I realized that this hiccup in my day would require a change to plans on my original itinerary.

I opened the door and re-entered the house, and I placed the note down on the kitchen counter with my purse as I looked at the clock. I did not wear a watch, as when I retired, I gave up assiduous time maintenance.

"I have two hours. What do I prepare? What do I have?"

I opened the fridge, unsure of what I was looking for.

"Lemonade," I said with confidence. "I will make fresh lemonade."

This reminded me of long summer days. I gathered several bright yellow lemons from the vegetable drawer. Then I went to my cabinet and grabbed a large glass pitcher. I began to gather all the necessary ingredients. As I cut and hand squeezed the lemons, I could not help but wonder about the next step—steps in a relationship that were common but uncommon to me. I also pondered the words on his card.

"We are all strangers until introduced," I thought as I paraphrased his words. "That is very deep and very personal," I thought as I considered the depth of his words.

My comfort zones were very distinct and defined. I did not deviate from them. I now found myself in uncharted territory. I was uncomfortable, but not so much so as to prevent my anticipation of the picnic.

Once the lemonade was made, I ascended my stairs to my bedroom to pick out an appropriate outfit. What appropriate was, I did not yet know.

"A dress. No, shorts. A dress would be awkward to sit in at a picnic," I said as I rifled through my closet, pushing aside item after item.

After I changed and descended the stairs in a pair of navy shorts and a white polo shirt, I rehearsed what I would say. I previewed what I would do on the anticipated date.

I gathered the pitcher that I had covered with plastic wrap, and walked out the door. As I walked up the path and into the woods, the birds scattered around me as I entered the domain that few others entered. The day was warm and bright. The sound of summer locusts off in the distant field became louder as I meandered through the path that was beaten down by the deer. I stepped out of the shaded woods that were buffered by the crowded trees and into the opening to the field spotted with purple, pink, and orange wild flowers that pierced through the monotone canvas of the pale yellow grass. Off in the distance, butterflies of several colors stood out against the light blue backdrop.

"I hope he means this field," I said to myself with a laugh, revealing my anxiousness.

I continued to walk down the path until I reached the spot where I imagined he would be. This was the only clearing in the field where he had taken his photographs, and it had the greatest proliferation of butterflies. Here also stood a small patch of ground shielded by a large lone oak tree. The tree was so massive that it shaded the ground beneath, preventing the normal ground cover of the surrounding area to grow.

Off in the distance, I could see Francis' tall frame. His back was turned to me. I noticed a blue cotton blanket on the ground and a picnic basket off to the side.

I continued to walk silently toward him. I did not want to draw attention to myself. I wanted to observe his movements, relish the moment, and capture a mental picture for posterity. I didn't remain unnoticed for long, however. He turned and saw me walking the narrow path through the tall grass towards him.

"Sophie," he called out as he walked toward me with that same bright smile that could illuminate the darkest of nights.

I did not respond. I merely smiled and continued to walk toward him. I had coached myself to act appropriately coy and not over anxious, although in my heart, I was a 15-year-old at her first dance.

As the distance between us shortened, a strong breeze interrupted the quiet, still framing of the moment. Specs of dry hay flew off the slender stalks, releasing a soft visual movement as the grass leaned and straightened with the direction of the wind.

The stack of paper that sat on the meticulously placed blanket vehemently lifted and took flight, off and into the field.

"Oh no," I gasped as Francis leapt forward in an attempt to catch his treasured photographs. "Get those ones; I'll go after these ones over here," I yelled out as I turned a sharp right and ran into the tall enveloping grass.

Within a single moment, I recognized the image in one of the photographs. It was a large Monarch butterfly in motion, moving with the wind. I ran toward it as I detached from the current and real world.

"Sophie, RUN, RUN. Don't look back," Lee frantically screamed out to me as her voice cut through the tall grasses like a sickle. I turned and saw the stranger grab her around the waste as her legs kicked forward. The man's hand stretched around her mouth, preventing her from speaking to me further, in fact, ever again.

Suddenly, I was 10 again, reliving the day my sister Lee was abducted. We were walking home from Sunday school along the desolate dusty farm road. A dark colored sedan pulled up and a heavy woman wearing a Sunday dress—a stranger—held a brown, crumpled bag out the window.

"Come here, girls. I have some candy for you," she called out to us.

I froze with fear as Lee walked toward the car, placing several feet between us. To this day, I know in my heart that she did this to allow me to gain ground and escape the predators.

As I stood staring at my older sister walking back toward the strangers' car, I could see the driver get out and run around the back of the car and grab her.

Her command for me to run was like a starting pistol for a track race. As soon as she released this directive, I reacted.

I ran into the tall golden refuge of the grass. The grass cut my feet, exposed and unprotected by my Sunday morning sandals. The skin of my legs split from the sharp caning of the stalks as I desperately ran into them.

"Toward the butterflies," I whispered aloud or so I thought. I ran toward the fluttering diaphanous movement of the butterflies that seemingly guided me away from the terrifying scene that was indelible to the rest of my life. I ran. I did not stop until I reached our farm.

Lee never returned from the dirt road that led home. She was never found.

Suddenly, I realized that the wind had stopped and the photo that I was chasing had collapsed onto the grass behind me. I stopped and wiped the tears from my face before I turned to see if Francis had observed my descent into my childhood nightmare.

He did. He was quickly walking toward me. "Sophie, are you okay. I have all the photographs," he called out to me.

He reached me and held out his arms, placing his hands on mine.

"Are you okay?" he asked in a very sympathetic and concerned voice.

"Yes, I am fine," I replied too abruptly to be convincing. "I got confused for a moment there." This was all I could say as I attempted to brush off the incident and control the damage that was already done.

I was visibly shaken. He did not know what to say. He placed a large protective hand gently onto mine and led me back to the picnic blanket, leaving the Monarchs behind me, and leaving Lee behind me once again. The summer and the return of the beautiful, fragile winged angels reminded me of the sacrifice my older sister had made for me. She had always taken care and mothered me. I learned over the years to embrace the warm, caring, protective nature that she showed during her short life, and not the ultimate sudden violent unrest she faced.

I cut short the picnic with Francis, as I could not bring myself to mentally move onto trivial conversations in fear of disrespecting the mental shrine that I had placed around the now sacred incident.

Chapter Three
Chrysalis

The rush of the day was wearing on my body as I did every imaginable chore in a frenetic time frame. I was feeling the soothing effects of the farm on my psyche as I entered the drive and began the ascent to the house.

As I pulled up to the door I noticed a bouquet of flowers that had been placed on my doorstep. I smiled and felt once again the warm rush of pleasure that accompanied the thoughts of Francis.

I leapt out of the car, ignoring the bags upon bags that remained inside. I quickly pulled out the note card nestled in the large arrangement of soft, muted water colored flowers. The card read,

Tonight is the gallery opening. I will not accept denial, Sophie. The series is called IN SUMMER'S FLIGHT, Butterflies at Fenn Farm. It is only fitting that the matriarch be present. AND besides, I would love to introduce you around.

With all my thoughts,

F.R

I smiled and held the card to my chest. The days following the picnic were taxing for me, but his quiet persistence abated me from my flighty instincts.

"Of course I will attend, Mr. Rogers," I said aloud. As I picked up the arrangement, my spirits soared and the world seemed to swirl around my head. I entered my house and closed the door, placing the bouquet on the table.

"Damn, the groceries," I said as if the rest of the day had already evaporated. I looked up at the clock to see how much time I had to get ready.

The hands unfortunately read 4:00. I rushed back outside and grabbed the bags to quickly bring them into the house and into their proper places.

*****

As I entered the gallery, I looked for Camille and a table that would offer me a beverage.

"God, I hope they are serving wine." My eyes scanned the large non-descriptive gallery with clusters of people standing around with social grace. The white walls and floor gave a perfect backdrop to Francis' brightly colored photos. I scanned the room desperately for the table of food and beverages.

"I hope Camille is here. I really don't want to stand here alone looking longingly at Francis or his photos," I thought to myself. My eyes caught one of the photos as I searched the room. I stopped and walked over to the photo.

It was of a white framed house and a woman in the field. Like a quick piercing slap on my cheek, I recognized that it was me in the picture on the day of the picnic as I ran into the field.

"This can't be me! Yes, it is!" I said to myself as I stepped in closer in complete disbelief and denial at what I was seeing.

"This is from the picnic!" I was suddenly overwhelmed with anger. My face immediately reddened as I tried to contain the swell of emotion ready to capsize my composure.

"Sophie, come meet my benefactors." I felt a soft touch on my shoulder as I heard Francis' voice. I turned to face a group of seven people with a bright, happy, civil demeanor.

"Hello, Hello Francis." I tried desperately not to embarrass myself or bring unwanted attention to the photo in dire fear that someone would ask me about it. Just then, Francis spoke up.

"This is Sophie. All of these breathtaking butterflies were photographed on her beautiful farm. She cultivates a butterfly field behind her house," he said.

"Oh, how lovely," someone replied.

I just stood and squeezed my ring housed on my finger as if the repetitive twirling of the band would keep me preoccupied.

"Sophie is like a mother to me," Francis said.

"*Sophie is like a mother to me?* Did he just say what I think he said?" I wondered. A cold shock overwhelmed me. The softly fitted black cocktail dress with the satin black pumps I was wearing somehow made me feel stupid and set up.

"I couldn't have heard him correctly. Mother? M O T H E R?" a crazy hysterical voice said in my head; I was convinced that the group could hear me as the word "mother" resonated in my mind. I did not know what to say as the group waited eagerly for me to share something insightful and perceptive.

"Do I say, 'Francis, can we speak privately?' Do I excuse myself?" I thought of the possible response that I could give before my composure broke completely.

"Oh, that is too sweet…and unnecessary. My farm is amazing. Oh, I am sorry, I must excuse myself for a minute; my friend just walked in. She is looking around for me. I must let her know I am here." I spoke with a choked voice, as I had to clear my throat mid-way.

Camille had not yet arrived. I made haste to the door, opened it, and kept walking until I passed the windows of the gallery. I then ran to my car as tears streamed down my face. I drove home with my eyes fixed forward, numb to my surroundings. Once again, I exhaled when I reached the drive to the farm. I felt the calming environment welcome me home.

As I exited the car and entered the house, all I thought was, "How could I have been so stupid? I thought he was attracted to me. What is wrong with me?"

As I opened the refrigerator door, I reached for the bottle of Chardonnay that was chilled and waiting for an occasion such as this.

I uncorked it and poured myself a drink.

As I sat at the table looking out the window, my reflection in the window was all I could see. I could not see past myself and into the yard where beauty lied. I could not see past my reflection and past the yard to the trees, or the sky, or the hundreds of stars that occupied the night.

This night, I could only see my reflection in a cast of self-doubt and self-wallowing. I could not understand how I had misread the relationship so drastically. I could not believe that a person I thought highly of would exploit my emotions in such a way.

"Granted, Francis did not know why I was crying in the field, but hell, he knew I was upset. How could he use that photograph without asking me?" I questioned and chastised everything about Francis and the time we spent together.

Soon, the alcohol deflated my energy and I lumbered up the stairs to strip myself of the frivolous frock that I had thought showed my youthfulness so confidently only hours earlier. I thought of how my ascension of these steps at this hour was the so completely opposite in so many ways to what it had been earlier. "I ran up these steps with anticipation to get ready for this opening. Now, I am dragging myself up the same stairs, trying to forget it ever happened." I shook my head in disbelief at the entire affair.

Soon, the events faded as my eyes shut out the circumstances, comments, scenes, and players.

I woke to the sound of the birds singing their usual songs at this early hour. I opened my eyes and saw the dress that lay in a pile like a black shroud. I sat up for several minutes to an hour looking out at the garden. Rabbits, squirrels, and chipmunks showed themselves to the world, moving forward with life. I looked at the flowers and trees as they evolved each second, growing, living through the natural cycle. I noticed the rose that was a mere bloom weeks ago and was now full and gorgeous, open at its peak. Then it struck me like the blindsiding comment from Francis the night before.

"The beauty surrounding me is beautiful at every stage of its life. Even trees in winter are beautiful; they contrast the white backdrop of winter. My roses are at summer's peak, yet I thought they were gorgeous at first bud." I began to realize how fortunate I was to have my wondrous surroundings and how the seasons parallel those of my own life and aging process. My eyes opened and soon, my attitude about Francis also changed.

"Francis does not realize that he hurt me." I thought about the picnic. "I did not tell him why I was upset. I made it seem as though I was okay."

I even reconsidered the mother comment. "He is 20-something years younger. He doesn't know what he is missing," I said with a confident smile, as I was back to my confident self. Although I admitted, "Mother nature may have helped out."

*****

The sugar slowly drifted to the bottom of the pitcher and swirled around the tea bags as I stirred the tea that had been sitting in the bold summer sun. I was preparing tea and making a salad with the fresh vegetables from my garden for Camille and me. She had called earlier that day on an unusual impromptu note, asking if she could stop by.

"I am sure she wants to get the dirt on Francis and why I left the opening," I said to myself as I thought about the reasons for her sudden call.

I was fine with the current status of the non-relationship. I was at a point of homeostasis with my age, my mortality, and my surroundings.

As I snapped the blue and yellow linen tablecloth over on the café table that sat outside in the yard, I carefully placed the plates, cutlery, and glasses around the vase containing an assortment of English roses that were just clipped from the garden. The smell brought a sweet scent like that of bottled rose perfume to the table and surrounding area. As I folded the linen napkins, I contemplated the liaison between Francis and me.

"I wonder why he has not taken me out," I asked myself as I had already done countless times. We had many encounters, but they were always confined to the farm. We had not been out, per se.

As I began to tie a white ribbon around the napkin, I heard the stones of the driveway beckoning. Camille's car was coming up the drive.

As I went to greet her, she popped open the trunk of her car. As the car door swung open out she jumped in a pair of faded jean capris, Crocs, and a loose fitting linen button down shirt. Her garb was as casual and comfortable as her personality.

"I come bearing gifts," she proclaimed as she pulled me into her, her arms enveloping my frame.

"Oh, good, it's about time you do something nice for me other than introduce me to men." I laughed as I spoke. No sooner did I get out the first word of my next sentence did she pull out a picture from her trunk. I stopped speaking and moved toward her trunk.

"I was told by Mr. Rogers to give this to you." She turned around a picture: a white frame around a breathtaking picture of a butterfly emerging from its chrysalis. The photo was as he described his work: black and white with hand-colored interpretation.

"That is beautiful," I said, as the original words I attempted to speak escaped me.

"There is a card," she said as she handed me the familiar bright orange colored envelope. "Go on, read it. Then tell me what it says." She looked at me with a hint of naughtiness.

I opened the card thinking, "Déjà vu." The card read,

Sophie, I feel in some way that I must have offended you and for that I am truly sorry. This is my favorite photo from the series. I titled it Chrysalis. When the Monarch is ready to make its way into the world, the chrysalis color changes into the beautiful colors of the Monarch. You are as beautiful inside and out. I hope you enjoy it.

Yours Truly,

F.R.

I couldn't immediately comment. I took the picture from Camille's hands and walked over to the chair. I sat and placed the art on my lap. I stared at it for a few minutes before Camille interrupted.

"What did he say, for God's sake?" She grabbed the card from my hand. "Oh my, that is really deep," she said, not knowing the implication of the words or of the present.

I responded to her, "It's amazing. That is all I can say. It is me, it is this farm, and it is Lee."

With this last comment, I asked that we spend our time talking about us and not Francis or the photo. Camille was a very close and longtime friend; sensing my emotional response to the photo, she did not pry.

We talked, laughed, and pointed out various spots of the yard and woods that showcased the beautiful summer we were having—the beautiful summer of my life.

Fall Change

Chapter One
Prejudice of Death

The sweet smell of Gardenias filled my room and mind with memories of summer. I could not resist spraying another pump before putting away the fragrant room spray. When the sun's stamina waivered and the days were robbed of light, my mood could not help but follow. Although the picturesque displays of autumn's roasted colors were glorious, it always took me weeks to adjust to the loss of summer.

Each season brings a vast amount of work that needs tending too on this farm. The imperious winter requires all the flowers and bushes on the ground be cut back and mulched, especially the roses. I had been putting off cutting back the gardens, although the blooms had denied me.

"Today is the day," I sighed as I once again attempted to prepare myself for the removal of the remnants of summer. There was more to the change of seasons. I was feeling a change within myself. The energy I always relied on was not as prevalent.

As I walked through the house and out the door, I noticed a gaggle of geese overhead honking loudly as the they followed the lead bird in his tailwinds. I stopped and watched them fly overhead until they were past my view of the horizon.

The wind blew over the long flat pasture and into the tree line, sending multi-colored leaves into the air, then whirling and floating to the ground. The sky was unmistakably gray, ominous of a storm. I felt the damp chill from the last rain clouds that soaked the ground and matted the leaves, reconstituting them from their brittle state.

I struggled with the task at hand and decided that instead of cutting back my landscapes, I would take a walk before the rain set in once again. I decided to walk along the north side of the property today, for the promenade of aged oak and maple trees would surely life my spirits. With every step, I felt the aching of my knees, hips, and back.

"I hope I am not getting my first cold of the season," I thought as I stepped with a slower gate than usual. As I passed the barn that stood in proud vigilance of the original homestead, I noticed that the upper hayloft door was missing, for how long I did not know, as I had not walked this back route for some time.

"That is odd. I wonder how long this has been off the hinges," I thought as I inspected the area directly under the missing door.

I bent over to pick up the door that was in pieces from the long 20-foot descent. As I moved, a sharp stabbing pain ripped through my lower back causing me to stiffen and reach back with my right hand. As I slowly stood up, I heard a slight shuffling of sorts in the upper hayloft.

"There must be cats in there again," I conjectured as I headed toward the upper door leading to the hayloft. I slowly opened the old weathered doors that drown out any sounds foretelling of an uninvited guest.

I looked around at eye level, then to the ground. In front of me, I surveyed saucer-sized puddles of white-gray color. I walked over to the area that was littered with bird droppings. I looked up to the rafters thinking to myself, "This is one large bird."

To my amazement, quietly and motionless, perched on the high timber beam was a stoic barn owl, eyes open and fixated on my movements. I also froze.

"What is it doing in here?" I thought as I stared at the large bird in awe and amazement. Its white heart-shaped face was a beautiful contrast to the reddish brown wings.

The owl did not move, nor did it fly away; it just stared at me. I started to slowly back out of the barn, as I did not want to scare the bird. As I made my way backwards to the doors, I looked up at it one more time, certain that the next time I looked into the barn, it would be gone.

As I slowly closed the doors, I could not help but wonder why it hadn't flown away. I hoped that it was not injured. I did not want to find a dead barn owl inside the barn. As I returned to my walk, the thought of the owl and the story behind its residence in my barn engaged my imagination. It had been the first time I had seen one on the property, let alone in the barn itself.

I was but 25 yards into my walk when the cold and threatening clouds released a crisp, steady drizzle. I turned and walked back to the house. As I passed the barn, I could not help but peek inside to see if the owl was still there or if it had been a figment of my imagination, as I was still astounded by the vision of it.

I had left the large double doors slightly cracked open when I exited the last time, affording me easy visual access. As I slowly walked up to the doors and leaned in, there was the owl, still perched on the beam looking out the opening of the barn.

I walked away with a renewed interest in the change of the season and my lack of outside enthusiasm. Even the rain did not penetrate my lighthearted mood as I walked back to house to go online and do some research on the barn owl.

I entered the house and stopped at the window to look out at the large weathered barn, past the rain, through the splintered wood, and inside at the owl. I could not help but feel that the sudden appearance of the great white rapture was a strange foreboding portent.

Chapter Two
Falling Signs

Some cultures see the white barn owl as a sign of death, while others, good fortune and purity. I looked out at the barn as I read the words on my laptop. I also learned that the bird that had appeared was a female as evinced by her decorous feathers and spotted chest.

"Hmm, death or good fortune; that is bi-polar," I thought as I looked at my laptop with confusion. I was compelled to study the bird that was bringing an omen of some form to my life.

"As if my summer was not bad enough," I thought as I shook my head with lighthearted dismissal of my negativity.

I decided that the bird was bringing bad luck, as it was always displayed with a bad omen of sorts. My cell phone rang as I started to imagine a potential scenario of bad events that could befall me. I closed the site's page and noticed an e-mail that had been in my inbox for two weeks.

The e-mail was from Francis.

Sophie,

I want to invite you to have dinner with me and one of my favorite women in the world.

"Great, more embarrassment and insults," I thought as I prematurely drew a conclusion as to where Francis was going with this e-mail. I continued to read…

My daughter Grace is here for a weekend and I would love for you two women to meet. Let me know if you are up to it.

Always,

F.R.

His daughter? I didn't even know he'd been married before. My curiosity fell victim to a great wave of guilt. The e-mail was weeks old and it appeared, I am sure, to Francis that I had simply ignored him.

"Damn. What am I going to do now?"

Although I was hurt and had significantly been put in my place at the gallery opening, his actions and gift showed me that I may have acted impetuously. Since the event, as Camille and I referred to it, he had continued to call and send cards and other small gifts, demonstrating genuine affection, or mere tenacity. I still avoided contact with him as I constructed a barrier of reality, as I called it. I was older than he was and he showed only interest in friendship. To step into a platonic role with him would always make me feel inadequate.

I tried to decide what form of contact I should offer him. "Should I e-mail him and explain that I rarely check e-mails or just call him?"

"The owl!" I thought with great enthusiasm. "He would love to photograph the owl." I delighted in the thought of having such a great subject to divert his attention.

I reached for my cell phone and found his name in my call log. As the phone rang, I glanced out at the barn trying to conjure a plan to keep the bird in my barn long enough for him to come and photograph it. Much to my relief, Francis' voicemail intercepted the call.

"Francis, it's Sophie. I just today read your e-mail about the dinner invite two weeks ago. I apologize for my lack of attention to my e-mails. I hope you can forgive me. I want to invite you over to the farm to view and photograph a magnificent sight. A large female barn owl has taken up residence in my barn. If your daughter is still in town, please bring her along. I hope to hear from you."

Hope emanated from me and my voice was positive. I placed the phone in my pocket and rifled through my drawers looking for my binoculars to view the owl.

Once I found them, I headed to the barn, not realizing that I had left the phone in my pocket. I was thankful that it rang 20 feet from the barn, alerting me then and not while I was inside the barn marveling at the owl.

"Hello."

"Sophie, it's Francis. How are you?" The voice was pleasant and welcoming.

"Great and you?" I asked.

"I would love to see and photograph the owl. Thank you for the invitation. My daughter, Grace, is still here. We will accept your invite," he said.

I wanted to make a joke or a comment about the lack of diplomacy on my part regarding not replying to his invitation, but I did not want to bring it up for fear that it would backfire. The pause was obviously causing him to continue speaking without my response.

"The invitation is still good, isn't it?" he questioned with a hint of disappointment in his voice.

"Yes, definitely. When is good for you? I would make it sooner rather than later, as I am not sure how long she will be in my barn."

My encouragement was successful. He immediately responded, "We will be there later today, around two o'clock."

"That is perfect; I look forward to meeting the both of you." I disconnected the call, turned, and headed back to the house to prepare. I stopped short and turned back around. "Wait, I better check to see if the bird is still there," I thought in horror that with the luck I'd had lately, it will have been gone and this whole invite will appear to be some desperate ploy by an aging predator.

"But if it is gone, I will have to call him back and cancel." I stopped and turned back toward the house again. "I would rather be surprised with them here than disappointed alone."

I walked briskly back to the house with a plan in my head.

*****

Francis and Grace both visited the barn owl and me several times that week. I found great pleasure in welcoming Grace onto the property and introducing her to the various varieties of trees and plants that inhabited the grounds.

I have always embraced the French philosophy, *je ne regrette rien,* in not regretting the past. The past always held dual meanings that one would tend to remise about as sorrowful events but carried with the sorrow was often change, opportunity, and growth. As my body matured, so did my philosophies on aging and change. The lessons of this past summer ignited another spiritual growth spurt within me.

I wanted to walk back into the barn one more time before the darkness beckoned the owl to make her exit. I had come to learn her habits over seven days of study.

The rain fell steadily this day, soaking the leaves against the ground, forming a vast colorful decoupage. The spongy ground that surrounded the barn required high steps to avoid losing one's shoes or boots in the muck. The farm had been called Fenn Farm since 1887 when the original owners came over from England. A fenn is a path of ground that is saturated with water. This was a very fitting name for the grounds, as they contained several natural springs that fed the grass and hay all year round. When I purchased the farm decades ago, I found several documents from the original owners that referred to the original name. I proudly honored this title.

The cold drizzle of rain created enough moisture to show my breath as I trudged to the barn entrance. I slowly turned sideways and ducked through the door that I had left ajar.

"There she is," I said as I looked up at the pure white feathers of her back. I looked at the ground underneath her perch to see what she had been hunting at night. There was no evidence or skeletal remains yet. I knelt down and watched her movements until the light no longer peeked through the slats of the boards of the barn.

With a sudden drop and then a swoosh, her nearly four-foot wingspan opened up as she pushed off from the beam and gracefully glided downward and through the hayloft door. Only after she was outside did she flap her wings, and with two or three flaps of these aerodynamic wings, she was out of sight.

I stood up and walked over to the bottom of her perch to take a closer look at her droppings and remains. There was no fur, feathers, or bones. If she was hunting and eating normally, she would consume the mammals or birds then discard their bones.

"I hope she is not ill," I thought as I grew very concerned for my new resident.

I made my way back to the house. Once in the field, I turned and looked to the night sky to see if I could see her off in the distance. I could not. For no impetus, I looked down toward the field and saw her on the ground. I stopped my breath and my heartbeat jumped as I took several large leaps closer to the field.

"Why is she on the ground? Was she sick like I thought?" I strained my eyes to look into the dusk sky, trying to see her movements.

Just as soon as I spotted her on the ground, her great wings opened and lifted her body off the ground and back into graceful flight.

I exhaled with relief as I thought, "She is okay." I could not overcome a disconcerting feeling, however, that the intimidating creature was not well.

She circled the dark sky as though she were an angel in flight. There appeared to be something hanging from her feet. As she flew closer to the barn, I could hear the screaming of a small animal. I ran as fast as the ground would permit back to the barn and wedged myself in between the large doors and pried them open as quickly as I could. She had already arrived back with her prey. Though I could hear the high-pitched cries of a small animal, I could not decipher what kind of animal it was. Once inside the barn, the cries grew louder and more audible.

On the ground lay a small ball of fur, legs out straight, shaking as if it were dying.

"Oh my god, I screamed as I dove to the ground to pick it up." As I scooped up the small, bloodied, limp body, I could see that it was a kitten—a small grey and white kitten no more than six weeks old. Unfortunately, there were many litters of stray cats that would give birth in the barn. The kittens rarely left the barn at this early age, unless the mother failed to return.

"Shh," I said as I attempted to soothe the kitten while I tried to maintain enough composure to think rationally.

Tears naturally swelled up in my eyes at the sight of the young life struggling to survive. The horrific cry of suffering from pain was unnerving. I could see large, deep gashes where the owl's claws dug into the kitten's body. I did not look up at the owl. I did not have time. I unzipped my jacket and brought the bleeding kitten to my stomach in an attempt to keep it warm. I grabbed my shirt and pulled it up and over the kitten, forming a hammock to shelter it. Its head bobbed limply and fell to the side away from me. The tiny blue eyes of the kitten were barely open.

All I could say was, "Shh," as I walked as quickly as I could through the muck, trying not to toss around the listless body. Once I reached the house, I grabbed my car keys and my cell phone and walked quickly to the car. My best friend Camille's sister was a country veterinarian. I struggled to speed dial her number while holding the kitten that had now saturated my shirt with blood and while fumbling for the ignition key.

Each subsequent hour was indistinguishable from the one before it. I picked up Camille and we drove straight to her sister Karen's house. Once inside, she took the kitten from my arms and rushed it downstairs. Camille found me a clean tee shirt and sat me down at the kitchen table with one of many cups of tea. After many hours, much stress, and high tension, Karen appeared at the top of the step, wiping her hands with a towel.

"You can come see her," she called out to both of us.

Camille and I followed her down the steps, eager to see the kitten. There on the stainless steel table lay the kitten on her side, still asleep from the anesthesia. Her long grey fur was shaved back to the skin, exposing line after line of black stitches that circled from her back to her tiny belly.

"Wonder why the owl dropped her?" I said to Karen.

"Normally, a barn owl wouldn't drop its prey," she explained. "How long has the owl been in your barn?" she asked.

"About a week. I have been watching her neurotically. I don't see her eating. There are no bones or fur, or signs of a carcass," I explained, hoping to get some answers.

"She may not be well. Keep watching her and let me know. As far as the kitten is concerned, I will watch her for the next couple of days. It was a blessing and good fortune that you saw her being taken and followed her back to the barn. She would have died within the hour if not for you, Sophie." I stroked the kitten's fur as Karen spoke these reassuring words.

"Now you have a kitten," Karen commented.

"Now I have a kitten? Great," I sarcastically spoke to myself. I never wanted to bring a cat into my cherished wildlife sanctuary at the farm. Flashbacks of Camille's cat stealing the bunny flashed back as I thought about a cat on my farm.

"Can I come back tomorrow to see her?" I asked.

"Most definitely," Karen replied. "For now, she will sleep, and we will check on her in the morning."

I left the house feeling tired and overwhelmed. I began searching the archives in my mind for a home for the now special kitten. All I could think of was Francis' daughter, Grace. They did not have a pet, and after I had spent every day this week with her, she seemed to me to be the perfect match.

As I left Karen's home, I called Francis. "Francis, how do you feel about cats?"

Chapter Three
Interweaving Foliage

I lifted my head to the sound of a faint knocking. I sat up and heard it again before I realized what time it was and the fact that I had overslept from the frenzied events of the prior night.

I had completely forgotten that Francis was bringing Grace over to spend the day sketching the owl. We had agreed to have an art lesson that day.

I jumped out of bed and ran down the stairs. Standing on the doorstep was Grace, with a back at toe, peering into the window. I opened the door and gave her a big hug as I spoke, "Grace, it is so nice to see you."

"My dad said you have a kitten for me. Can I see it?" she asked immediately without acknowledging my greeting.

"The kitten is not ready yet." I tried to gingerly explain, "She has a cut that needs to heal. She is at my friend's house getting better. Once she is well enough, I will bring her to your house." I did not consider the possibility that the kitten would not live.

"Okay. I can't wait to see it. My Dad said she is grey and white. I am going to call her Fenn, after the name of your farm," she proudly announced.

This sentiment overwhelmed me with a warm rush of purpose and meaning. "That is perfect, Grace. She fits that name," I replied. "I am going to run up and change. Why don't you peek into the barn at the owl and I will meet you up there."

She agreed to go to barn and get ready to sketch and I ran up the steps to brush my teeth, pull my hair back, and change.

I had just brushed my teeth and was pulling out a pair of jeans when I heard the door fly open and slam into the wall. I stopped and stood up.

"Sophie, come quick! The owl is on the ground!" Grace screamed with a tone of sheer panic and fear.

"Oh my God, the owl *was* sick," I thought as I dropped the jeans and ran down the steps to Grace. By the time I got to the door, she had already left the house and was running back up toward the barn. I ran after her.

As I entered the barn, I could see one white wing stretched out and bent on the ground. The beautiful heart-shaped face was down on the ground and the other wing was folded inward toward her body.

I motioned with my hand for Grace to stay back, as I slowly walked toward the owl. I did not have a positive feeling. The owl was in an unnatural state that suggested death. The owl did not move as I walked closer to her. I knelt down and the owl did not move. I reached out and touched her body. It was warm and soft. Still, there was no movement. I reached out to the long white wing that was extended and folded it back to its natural resting state and turned her over.

There was blood coming from her beak. It was smashed, apparently from the fall. The skin around her eyes was rigid and the gold and black round eyes glazed over in a stoic stare.

Grace slowly walked toward me as she cried, "Is she dead? Sophie, is she d e a d?" sobbing between each syllable.

"Yes, Grace, I'm afraid she is." All I could think of was the horrible environment I had brought this young girl into. I asked her over to witness the beauty and life of the barn owl and here she was witnessing the horrific sight of the creature's corpse. I did not know what to say or how to explain or console the young girl who was now sobbing and burying her face in her hands. I placed the owl into an empty wheelbarrow and walked over to Grace, struggling with my body's actions and for words.

As soon as I reached her, she leapt forward and wrapped her arms around my waist. She held me tight as she cried; I stroked her hair and back. I did not speak to her, nor did she speak to me. Tears were also flowing from my eyes. We embraced each other for solace and comfort. Our actions proved superior to words.

After several minutes, I convinced her to return to the house. I attempted to explain to her that life has a cycle. Barn owls only lived to be two or three years old. I told a tale of how the great white owl lived a special life and came into the barn for a special place to die. As I creatively wove the inspiring words together, I started to actually ponder what I was telling her.

All living beings, large and small, have a birth, a life, and a death, and time was elusive and precious. Fenn Farm was a profoundly special place that brought a magical calmness to all who inhabited or embraced it.

"Our owl, Grace, spent her last hours doing what she loved and what she did best: soaring the night sky scanning the grounds and living free and awesome," I explained to her.

Francis came early, given the traumatic events. Once he heard and saw the state we were both in, he comforted us and told me he would take Grace home and return later if I needed his company. The gesture was standard thoughtful Francis; however, I wanted to go visit the kitten—the kitten that would be a loving companion to Grace, and the same kitten that escaped the claws of the owl on her last night of flight. It all made sense.

The chain of events was unpredictable, unscripted, yet auspicious as much of life was.

Chapter Four
Full Circle

The kitten grew strong and the wounds healed. Karen removed the stitches to reveal that new fur was already growing back around the scars. It was time to take the kitten to Grace. The last week was brought into perspective with the death of the owl. I came to see her arrival, her week in my barn, and her death as good fortune instead of the stigma of bad luck or death.

Although the owl ultimately brought death, more importantly, it brought a great sense of purpose and fulfillment to my life. Grace and Francis were irreplaceable figures in my life. I was, in my own right, still settling into my third season of life, and the owl brought me great clarity of purpose.

I did not see the owl again after I placed her in the wheelbarrow. Francis agreed to remove her. It saddens me greatly to have my memory indelibly etched with the vision of her collapse and her broken wing. I struggled to replace this image with the one from hours earlier when she glided through the door of the barn and out into the darkening sky that seemingly illuminated her white feathers in flight.

My deep thought was refocused back to reality when Fenn meowed loudly from the carrier that I had placed on the passenger seat.

"Wow, Fenn, this is a far cry from the last time you were a passenger in this car," I spoke to her as I drove to Francis' home.

I did not have a chance to knock at the door before it swung open and Grace called out to her dad with excitement, "She is here; Sophie and Fenn are finally here, Dad! Hurry up!" Grace screamed back into the house at her father.

I had barely entered the house when she grabbed the carrier from me and placed it on the floor. She opened the door and gently removed the kitten, who immediately took to her as her new caregiver. I anthropomorphized that the small kitten somehow knew she was saved by a great fate and appreciated it.

As Grace and Fenn were bonding, Francis appeared and embraced me with a warm, loving hug.

"How are you with giving up Fenn? Are you sure you want to do it?" he asked, smiling and showing that Cary Grant smile once again.

"I think I can sacrifice her to Grace," I sarcastically replied.

"Follow me; I have something to give you," he said as he took me by the hand and led the way through his house, meandering between the furniture.

"More gifts? Are you still trying to court me F.R.? Because you can stop; you had me with the chrysalis photo," I mockingly replied.

"Just follow me, please," he said as he took me through a door leading to his studio. "Cover your eyes," he requested.

"Cover me eyes? Do I have to?" I tutted as I held my hands to my eyes.

Upon opening them, I saw perched on an old tree branch made into a stand my barn owl, wings spread, spanning all of her glorious eight feet or so. One leg was raised with its claws flared. The beak was repaired and open. It was so lifelike, you could almost hear her screeching.

"Francis, is this my owl?" I asked.

"Yes, I did remove her as you asked, but I could not dispose of such a magnificent creature. I hope you are not against me having her restored." His tone lowered as he awaited my response.

I did not speak; I turned to him and without thinking, driven by emotion, fell into his arms just as Grace had leapt into mine the day she found the owl.

We did not speak. I held him and he held me tighter. Our friendship, which was most important to me, had also come full circle with the presence of this once foreboding barn owl.

For the next decade of my life, I looked at the great white owl beginning her flight and was reminded of our own mortality, but above all, the role that Fenn Farm played during all of the seasons of our lives.

Breinigsville, PA USA
03 December 2010
250592BV00002B/1/P

9 781451 234794